BILLY AND THE MINI MONSTERS

Monsters on the Move

ZANNA DAVIDSON

Illustrated by
MELANIE WILLIAMSON

Reading consultant: Alison Kelly

Meet Billy...

Billy was just
an ordinary boy
living an ordinary
life, until

ONE NIGHT

he found

five

MINI
MONSTERS

in his sock drawer.

Gloop   Peep   Fang-Face   Captain Snott   Trumpet

Then he saved their lives, and
they swore never to leave him.

We give you
the Secret-Hairy-
Snot-Tooth Oath
of Devotion.

We're
awesome!

And
fun!

And
SCARY!

Are we
scary? I'm
not sure I'm
very scary.

One thing was certain –
Billy's life would never be
the same **AGAIN**...

Contents

Chapter 1

Moving Day

"It's moving day!" cried Captain Snott. "Hooray! We're going to the new house."

Mmm. These boxes are tasty.

"But what does the new house look like?" asked Peep.

"Will it have cheese?" asked Trumpet, anxiously.

MY NEW HOUSE

Attic
(Spooky. Full of spiders.)

Ruby's new room
(It's smaller than mine. Ha ha!)

Kitchen
(Full of cheese for Trumpet.)

"Yes, it will have cheese," said Billy. "I'll draw the house for you."

Pointy roof

Wonky chimney
(Not sure why it's wonky.)

My new room
(Next to the spooky attic.)

Mom and Dad's room

Living room

Big yard with a fish pond (Full of pond slime.)

Cellar
(REALLY spooky.)

"Everyone's really excited about the new house," said Billy. "Everyone except ME."

Reasons NOT to like the new house...

1. It's miles away from my friends
2. I have to go to a new school
3. It's full of spiders
4. I like my OLD house

"*We're* excited!" said the Mini Monsters together. They were thinking of all the things they could do in the new house.

"Where is the new house?" asked Peep.

Billy opened the map his dad had given him and pointed to the big circle that marked where their new house was.

OLD HOUSE

It's far away out in the country.

"There are lots of trees around it," said Billy. "And some of the fields even have COWS. We'll have to walk through COWPATS to get anywhere."

Billy looked at them all. "Maybe moving *will* be fun. And Mom did say that there's a boy and girl the same age as Ruby and me next door…"

"Of course it'll be fun," said Fang-Face, grinning, "because

WE'LL BE THERE!"

"*Please* can we go on the truck?" begged Trumpet.

"Okay," said Billy. "But only if you promise to stay in your box."

"We promise," said the Mini Monsters.

Billy carefully put the Mini Monsters into the packing box.

Have fun! I'll be in the car just ahead of you.

No chewing, Fang-Face.

Peep, don't be scared.

Trumpet, try not to toot. Have you had any cheese?

Then he taped up the box and wrote in big letters on the outside:

BILLY'S TOYS!

VERY IMPORTANT!

FRAGILE!

"Billy!" called his mom. "Come downstairs. We're leaving!" Billy took a last look around his bedroom. It felt strange to be going to a new house.

"But at least I'll have the Mini Monsters with me," he thought.

21

Chapter 2
The New House

Billy watched as the movers unloaded the boxes from the truck. But there was no sign of his box.

Where has it gone?

He tried asking his parents for help, but they were too busy unpacking.

I've lost my toy box.

We'll help you later.

"Why don't you and Ruby go and play outside?" said his mom. "Take your soccer ball."

"Come on, Billy!" said Ruby. "I want to explore."

"I can't find my Mini Monsters," said Billy. "I don't know what's happened to them."

25

OR... maybe they've been **STOLEN?**

"And you'll

NEVER

see them again!" said Ruby.

Billy felt a little like crying. "I knew moving was a bad idea," he said. And he kicked his ball as hard as he could.

It sailed over the hedge...

...and into the yard next door.

"I can't go next door," said Billy.

"Why not?" asked Ruby. "Are you scared?"

"No," said Billy, even though he *was* feeling a little scared.

He **crept** through a hole in the hedge.

There was his ball, and standing beside it was a boy his own age.

But the boy didn't say a word.
He just turned and ran back to
his house.

That night, Billy went to bed in his new bedroom. It felt empty and **STRANGE**, and he didn't like the way the ceiling sloped.

"I **hate** the new house," he thought. "The next door neighbor doesn't want to be my friend. And nothing feels right without the Mini Monsters."

As Billy closed his eyes, he wished as hard as he could that he was back in his old room and that everything was just how it used to be.

31

Chapter 3
Surprise!

The next morning, Billy was still worried about the Mini Monsters.

Then his dad came in, carrying a **STRANGE**, blue **SOMETHING**.

Morning, Billy!

"I've got a surprise for you," said Dad. "I bought this before we left our old house. I knew it was perfect for your new room."

"Wow!" said Billy, trying to sound excited. "Thanks, Dad."

"I bought it from the same place as your dresser," his dad went on. "That funny old consignment store."

Billy waited until his dad was gone, then he quickly got dressed and raced into Ruby's room.

Wake up! Wake up!

"You know how the Mini Monsters arrived in my dresser?"

"Yes," said Ruby, still half-asleep.

"Well, Dad's bought me a desk from the same shop."

Maybe the desk's got Mini Monsters in it too!

That's what I was thinking. Let's look!

Billy and Ruby searched ALL the drawers in the desk.

They looked **under** the desk.

Nothing!

They looked **behind** the desk.

Still nothing!

But...

Then, from the very back of the desk, they heard a…

…squeaky *little* voice.

Let me out!

44

Chapter 4
Sparkle-Boogey

Billy and Ruby looked at the speaking desk with open mouths.

"Of course I'm a monster," the voice replied. "What else would I be? A talking snail?"

We're trying to get you out, but the door's stuck.

"Maybe," Billy thought excitedly, "the new monster can help me find my Mini Monsters." He was also wondering what the new monster looked like.

Would it have horns,
like Fang-Face?

Or be hairy
like Peep?

Or be stretchy
like Gloop?

Or maybe it would
be a mixture...

Then: "Can you hurry up?" huffed the voice. "Because I'm getting hungry in here."

This is a very bossy monster.

Billy gave a final tug to the little door on the back of the desk. It pinged open and there stood…

Sparkle-Boogey!

"Wow!" said Ruby.

"I know," said Sparkle-Boogey. "Aren't I *beautiful!*"

"Oh yes," said Ruby.

Billy wasn't so sure, but he was too polite to say so.

What would you like to eat?

Glitter and boogeys.

"I think I've got some glitter in my room," said Ruby. "I'll just go and get it."

When Ruby came back, Sparkle-Boogey gulped down the glitter. "Yum," she said.

Yuck!

"You're very different than my other Mini Monsters," said Billy.

"There are others?" asked Sparkle-Boogey.

"Yes," Billy replied, his heart falling. "There's...

Peep,

Trumpet,

Fang-Face,

Captain Snott

and Gloop.

"But I lost them in the move. I'm not sure I'll ever find them again. I was hoping you might be able to help..."

"Does one of them wear a cape?" asked Sparkle-Boogey. "And does one of them look like a hamster with wings?"

"Yes," said Billy. "How did you know?"

Look out of the window.

"Wow!" said Ruby. "They're coming back. And I think they're flying your kite, Billy." Billy took one look out of his window and raced outside.

Billy grinned. His Mini Monsters
were coming home!

In the air...

There's Billy!

Steer the kite down, Trumpet.

How?

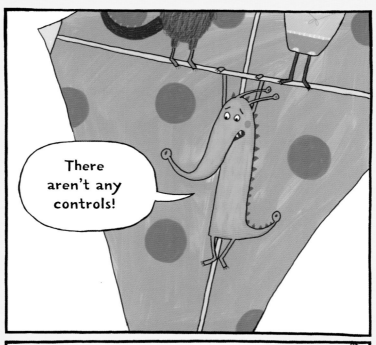

58

Chapter 5
Crash Landing

Billy could only watch as the Mini Monsters nosedived... straight into the yard next door.

Nooo!

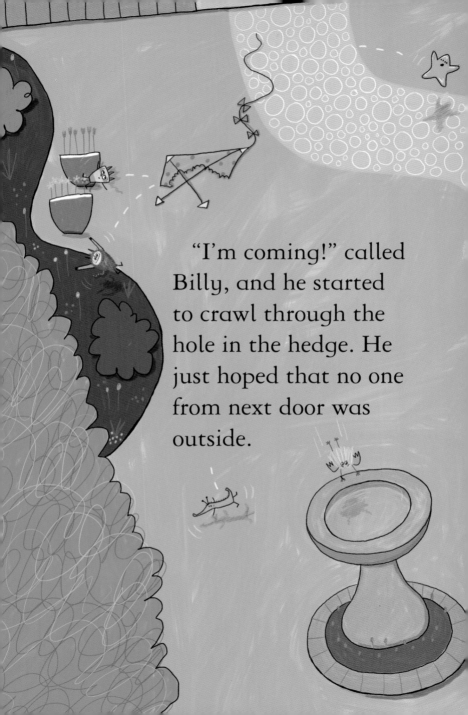

"I'm coming!" called Billy, and he started to crawl through the hole in the hedge. He just hoped that no one from next door was outside.

Billy quickly raced around, picking up all the Mini Monsters and putting them safely in his pockets.

I thought you were lost forever!

Then the sound of
loud footsteps
made him look up.

It was the boy again, with his sister.

"I was just, um, getting my kite," said Billy. "But I'll go now."

"My name's Ash," said the boy. "Sorry I ran away before. I get shy sometimes."

Would you like to come and play at our house?

"That would be great," said Billy. "I'll just go and check with my mom."

"Can your sister come and play too?" said the girl.

"I'll ask," promised Billy.

I'll be back soon!

Billy crawled back through the hedge, ran across the yard and up the stairs, two at a time. Then he took his Mini Monsters out of his pockets and grinned at them.

"I'm so glad you're back," said Billy.

"You won't believe the adventures we've had," said Captain Snott.

We fell out of the truck!

We hitched a ride on a car!

And crashed
into a hedge.

Peep was kissed
by a cow.

And then we
FLEW!

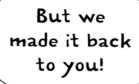

But we made it back to you!

Your room is even **BETTER** than your old one.

And this house is **awesome!**

"Hooray!" said Billy. "And I've got an even bigger surprise for you..."

Chapter 6

New Friends

"Billy," said Ruby. "Because you've already got five Mini Monsters, do you think Sparkle-Boogey could be mine?"

I'll be your monster!

"Definitely," said Billy, smiling.
"Do you want to come and see the
kids next door, while the monsters
get settled?" he asked Ruby.

"Yes!" said Ruby, already racing
out the door. "I'll just tell Mom."

I'll see you out there!

Billy looked at the Mini
Monsters but they seemed happy
chatting with Sparkle-Boogey.

"See you later," he said.

Peep fluttered over to him. "I like
it here," he whispered.

He thought of his new friends
next door, waiting for him. Then
Trumpet let out a loud…

TOOT!

Oh,
Trumpet!

Billy laughed. "Now
it definitely feels like
home," he said.

All about the MINI MONSTERS

CAPTAIN SNOTT →

LIKES EATING: boogeys.

SPECIAL SKILL:
can glow in the dark.

SCARE
FACTOR:
5/10

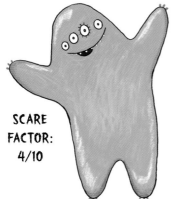

← GLOOP

LIKES EATING: cake.

SPECIAL SKILL:
very stre-e-e-tchy.
Gloop can also swallow his own
eyeballs and make them reappear
on any part of his body.

SCARE
FACTOR:
4/10

FANG-FACE →

LIKES EATING:
socks, school ties, paper, or
anything that comes his way.

SPECIAL SKILL:
has massive fangs.

SCARE
FACTOR:
9/10

TRUMPET →

LIKES EATING: cheese.

SPECIAL SKILL:
amazingly powerful
cheese-powered toots.

SCARE FACTOR:
7/10

(taking into
account his toots)

PEEP

LIKES EATING: very small flies.

SPECIAL SKILL: can fly (but
not very far, or very well).

SCARE FACTOR:
0/10 (unless you're afraid of
small hairy things)

SPARKLE-BOOGEY

LIKES EATING:
glitter and boogeys.

SPECIAL SKILL:
can shoot out
clouds of glitter.

SCARE FACTOR:
5/10 (if you're scared of
pink sparkly glitter)

Designed by Brenda Cole
Edited by Becky Walker
Cover design by Hannah Cobley
Digital manipulation by John Russell

First published in 2017 by Usborne Publishing Ltd., Usborne House, 83-85 Saffron Hill, London EC1N 8RT, England. www.usborne.com
Copyright © 2017 Usborne Publishing Ltd. AE